August 21, 2012

To my Dear Sisters

Beth

who I love so much.

always,

Pat

oo

xx

OINK

Arthur Geisert

Houghton Mifflin Company

Boston

For Tony and Leona Meier
Faulk County, South Dakota

Library of Congress Cataloging-in-Publication Data

Geisert, Arthur.
  Oink / Arthur Geisert.
    p.   cm.
    Summary: When their mother falls asleep, the baby pigs
sneak away, get into big trouble, and must be rescued.
    RNF ISBN 0-395-55329-6 PAP ISBN 0-395-74516-0
    [1. Pigs — Fiction.]   I. Title.
PZ7.G272401   1991   90-46123
[E] — dc20   CIP
                                   AC

Printed in Singapore
TWP 10 9 8

OINK

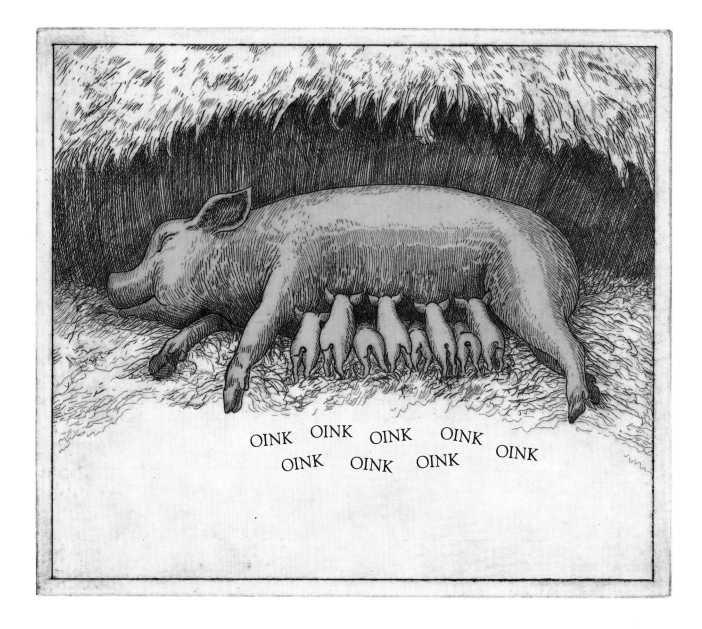

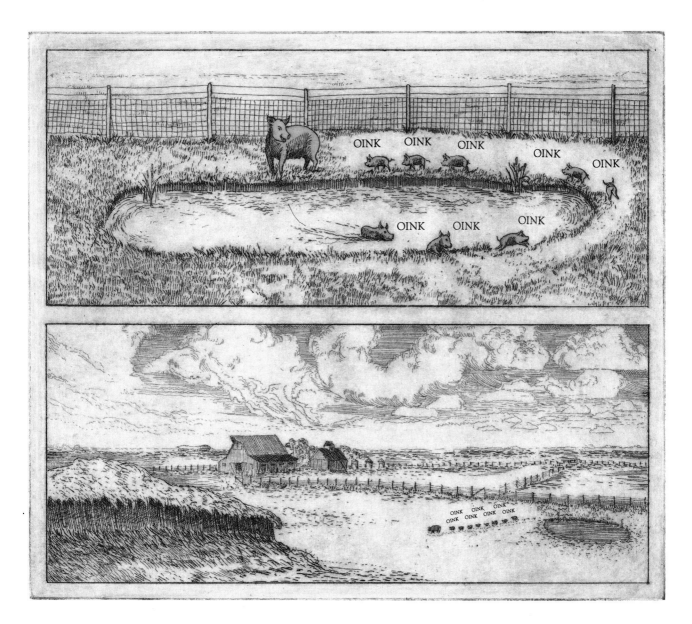

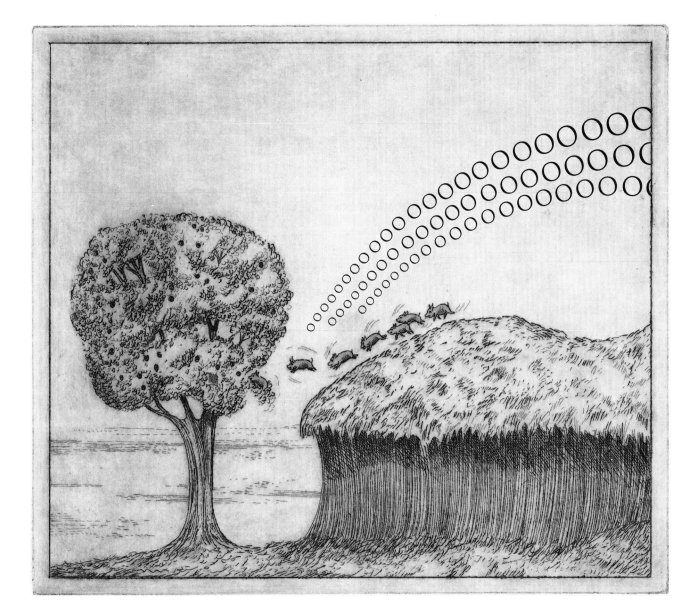

OINK